panda series

**PANDA books are for first readers
beginning to make their own way
through books.**

For Mary

Muckeen
The Pig

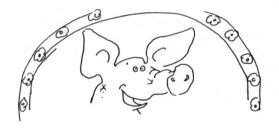

Words and pictures
• FERGUS LYONS •

THE O'BRIEN PRESS
DUBLIN

First published 1997 by The O'Brien Press Ltd.,
20 Victoria Road, Dublin 6, Ireland.
Tel: +353 1 4923333; Fax: +353 1 4922777
E-mail books@obrien.ie
Website www.obrien.ie
Reprinted 1998, 2000.

ISBN: 0-86278-528-6

British Library Cataloguing-in-Publication Data
A catalogue reference for this title is available
from the British Library.

3 4 5 6 7 8 9 10
00 01 02 03 04 05 06

The O'Brien Press receives
assistance from

The Arts Council
An Chomhairle Ealaíon

Typesetting, layout, editing: The O'Brien Press Ltd.
Cover separations: C&A Print Services Ltd.
Printing: Cox & Wyman Ltd.

Can YOU spot the panda
hidden in the story?

Once upon a time there was
a little pig called Muckeen.
He wasn't a clean little pig.
In fact, he was a very
dirty and untidy little pig.

But he was very happy.

He played mud pies
and digging for worms
for hours on end
in the farmyard.

And then at dinner time
Mrs Farmer would bring him a
big bucket of **sloppy stuff**
for his dinner.

He loved **sloppy stuff**
so much that as soon as he
heard the bucket rattling
he would **squeal**
and **dance**
with happiness.

When he started on his dinner
nothing would stop him
until he had eaten

every

    last

        little

            bit.

When he had finished
Muckeen would lick
his bucket clean
and only then would he
run off to play.

And so the days went by.

Then one day, at the end of
summer, Muckeen heard
Mrs Farmer say to Mr Farmer,
'I think Muckeen is
big enough now to take
to the market in the town.'

Muckeen was delighted
to hear this news.
He thought that
Mr Farmer was going to
take him to the town and
buy him a nice **hat**
and maybe an **ice cream**
as a special treat.

This excited Muckeen
so much that it almost
made him dizzy.

So he stretched out
on the grass
to have a little rest.

He closed his eyes and
was soon fast asleep.
Then he dreamed a
wonderful dream.

First, the dream was about
eating lots of **ice cream**
on a big mountain of
ice cream, with pink clouds
in the sky and snow
made of **ice cream**
falling all around.

Then, the dream was about
Muckeen showing off
in front of the chickens
in a new **hat**.

Muckeen woke up suddenly
with a squeal of fright
when a bee landed
on his nose.

Then he remembered that
Mr Farmer was going to
take him to the market
in the town for a
new **hat** and **ice cream**.
Muckeen felt happier
than ever.

But Mr Farmer was not
going to do this at all.

(He was going to

SELL Muckeen

in the town!)

It was a good job Muckeen
did not know this,
because if he did he would
never have gone with
Mr Farmer at all.
He would have stayed at home
playing mud pies.

The next morning
Mrs Farmer gave Muckeen
a good scrub until he was
pink and shiny and clean.

Then Mr Farmer, dressed in
his best, tucked Muckeen
under his arm and
set off for town.

Half way to the town
Mr Farmer met a man.
The man said, 'That's a
nice little pig you have there.
Will you give him to me?'

'Oh no!' said Mr Farmer. 'I'm
taking him to the market
in the town – and there
I'll sell him for **gold**.'

When Muckeen heard this
he didn't like the idea
one little bit.
He started to **squeal** and
squirm and **wriggle**
and **shove**
until he got free from
Mr Farmer's arms.

'I don't care about getting
a new hat!' said Muckeen
to himself.

'I don't even care
about ice cream!'

And back he ran
with a skip and a hop
along the road to the farmyard,
back to his mud pies
and the worms
he loved to dig for –
and the bucket of
sloppy stuff
for his dinner.

Mr Farmer ran after Muckeen,
waving a stick in the air.
But he was much too slow
and Muckeen was
much too fast.

When Muckeen got
to the farmyard,
what should he see
but a man walking
away with
HIS dinner bucket.

'This is too much!' said
Muckeen to himself.
'First, Mr Farmer wants to
sell me, and now that man
is taking away my
sloppy stuff!'

So with a brave **squeal** and
a mighty **leap** he knocked
the man over.

What was in the bucket but all of Mr and Mrs Farmer's **gold!**

At that moment Mrs Farmer
ran out of the house.
'Stop the thief,' she shouted.
'He has stolen the gold. He has
it in the slop bucket.'

She gave a great shout of joy
when she saw Muckeen.
He was sitting on the robber
and looking very pleased
with himself.

He had saved **his bucket**.
He didn't care about the gold!

When Mr Farmer got home,
Mrs Farmer told him how
Muckeen had stopped the
robber and saved
all their **gold**.
'Well, well, well,' said
Mr Farmer as he counted
the gold to make sure
all of it was there.

'Well, well, well,' he said again.
'Isn't Muckeen a very clever
little pig indeed!
I think we'll have to buy him
a nice **hat** and some
ice cream and let him
stay here for ever and ever –
and he can keep an eye
on our **gold**.'

Muckeen thought this was
a great idea, and off he went
to play mud pies
until dinner time –
when he would get
a grand big bucket of
sloppy stuff!

Well, did you find him?